THE INSIDE STORY!
STRUCTURE & FUNCTION

Written by Sharon Franklin

Illustrated by James Cloutier

GoodYearBooks

An Imprint of ScottForesman
A Division of HarperCollins*Publishers*

Acknowledgments
The author gratefully acknowledges the following people and groups:

Linda Brodie from Just Imagine! Children's Bookstore in Eugene, Oregon, for her support and assistance; the Eugene Public Library children's librarians for their generous help and interest in the project; Heidi Imhof for her suggestions and always inspiring philosophy of science education; Dick Lennox for his untiring spirit and hard work in getting this to disk; Mark Dow from the Willamette Science and Technology Center (WISTEC) for his reading of the manuscript; Tristan Franklin and Margot Volem for their work with the appendices and exuberant testing of experiments; Annie Vrijmoet and Nan Loveland for work on the original design and research; Bobbie Dempsey at GoodYearBooks for her support and editorial assistance; and to James Cloutier, with whom it was a distinct honor to share the journey of this project. Lastly, I thank my parents for continuing to try to understand just what it is I do for a living anyway.

GoodYearBooks

are available for most basic curriculum subjects plus many enrichment areas. For more GoodYearBooks, contact your local bookseller or educational dealer. For a complete catalog with information about other GoodYearBooks, please write:

GoodYearBooks
ScottForesman
1900 East Lake Avenue
Glenview, IL 60025

Illustrated by James Cloutier.
Copyright © 1995 Franklin & Cron Development Group, Inc.
All Rights Reserved.
Printed in the United States of America.

ISBN 0-673-36222-1 (Hardcover)

1 2 3 4 5 6 7 8 9 - DQ - 03 02 01 00 99 98 97 96 95

ISBN 0-673-36217-5 (Softcover)

1 2 3 4 5 6 7 8 9 - DR - 03 02 01 00 99 98 97 96 95

CONTENTS

SAFETY TIPS

1. **Pay attention to all WARNINGS.** They are marked with a label like this:

   Good safety practices are necessary for scientists of all ages.

2. **Wear your goggles.** They protect your eyes when mixing household or other chemicals.

3. **Don't be afraid to ask for help from adults.** Lots of adults like doing science experiments, mainly because they haven't had a chance to do any for a long time. Sometimes you may need their help, and sometimes you may want to invite adult family members to join in just for fun!

4. **Treat all substances as potentially hazardous**—for example, as flammable, corrosive, or toxic.

5. **Label all chemicals carefully, use them with adult supervision, and keep them out of the reach of young children.** Most of the chemicals in these investigations are common household substances such as vinegar, salt, and baking soda. Other chemicals are clearly marked with WARNING signs.

6. **Any time you are using the stove or matches, there is danger of fire. Make sure adults are present.**

7. **Be careful when using knives or other sharp instruments.** Wear goggles to protect your eyes.

WHAT CAN YOU DO WHEN AN EXPERIMENT "DOESN'T WORK"?

First of all, don't give up! Consider it a little challenge, and do some problem solving. Think out loud in your journal, asking yourself these questions:

1. What happened? What did you *expect* to happen?
2. Why didn't the experiment work like you thought it would?
3. What surprises did you find? What did you learn from the results?
4. What might you try differently next time? How could you test it out?

Remember: Often the most amazing and important scientific discoveries happen by accident—they are not planned. Mess around. Sometimes science is roll-up-your-sleeves, "thinking-on-your-feet" kind of work.

INTRODUCTION

What do elephants and arches, or domes and some viruses, have in common? What part does function play in the structural design of seed pods? What about sand dollars? They're just a few of the questions you'll begin to answer as you investigate the structure of bubbles, molds, birds, bridges, the human body, and more.

Grab your science journal and your loupe, and get ready to begin *The Inside Story!* A couple of Big Questions may help to guide your thinking as you work your way through the experiments in this book. Make some notes in your journal as you go along.

◆ What do you believe to be the overall goal of design?

◆ To whom would you give the Best Designer Award–to Mother Nature or to humankind, and why?

CHAPTER 1

WORLD OF CRYSTALS

What do sand, salt, ice, sugar, and diamonds have in common? That's right, they're all crystals! Some you eat; others you wear. Strange, but true. Grab your magnifying glass or jeweler's loupe and look at these crystals close up. Shake some salt and sugar on two pieces of black paper. Observe them carefully like a scientist. How are they alike? How are they different?

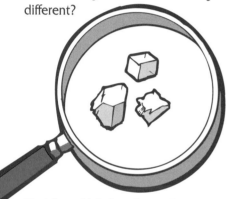

Sketch and label each one in your science journal. Are the crystals the same size? Describe what you see. What else do they remind you of?

Crystals—As Old As The Hills

Have you ever heard the expression "it's as old as the hills"? Whatever it is, you know it's pretty old. Crystals fit this description very well. Long ago, as the earth formed, the materials that composed it were very hot. As these liquid materials cooled, crystals formed.

Crystals are still growing in solutions today. Crystals need room to grow perfect shapes, and to grow large they need slow cooling or slow evaporation. Well-developed crystals have smooth, flat surfaces and sharp edges. Look for mirrorlike faces in the alum crystals you will grow and observe with your loupe.

Crystallography is the scientific study of crystals. Who knows, maybe you'll be a crystallographer when you grow up! (Warning: You'll probably need to spell the word from time to time.)

DIAMONDS ARE FOREVER

A diamond is so hard that only another diamond can scratch one. The Cullinan is the largest diamond ever found. It weighed 1 1/2 pounds and was cut into many large and small diamonds. Visit a jewelry store and watch the jeweler cut a stone. Then custom design a diamond ring in your journal. It won't cost a thing!

ROTATE AND FLY THROUGH

Did you know there are sophisticated computer programs that can draw, project the hidden lines, and rotate 3-D images of geometric shapes like those in some crystals? How do you think architects, artists, and surgeons make use of these programs?

EXPERIMENT 1: ROCK CANDY

SUPPLIES
goggles
1/2 cup water
1 to 2 cups granulated
  sugar
wooden spoon
tablespoon
a clean glass jar with lid
tweezers
small plastic bag

WARNING ! SUGAR SYRUP CAN GET VERY HOT. ASK AN ADULT TO HELP YOU WITH THIS NEXT PART.

1. Put on your goggles. Measure the water into a small saucepan and bring it to medium heat. Slowly add sugar to the water, one spoonful at a time, stirring each spoonful until it dissolves.

> Heating the water causes the water molecules to move farther apart and politely make room for more sugar, making it a SUPERSATURATED solution. That's why hot water can hold more sugar than cold water.

2. Record in your journal how many spoonfuls of sugar you add until no more will dissolve. When you reach this point, don't add any more sugar. The liquid should be a thick syrup. Don't stir it any more.

3. Carefully remove it from the heat and let it cool in the pan for a minute.

4. Pour a little of the solution carefully into the lid of the jar.

5. In a short period of time, little crystals will begin to form. Pick out the six biggest and put them in a jar. Cover them with solution.

6. Cover the jar with a plastic bag to keep it clean. Put the jar in a spot where it will not be bumped or moved, but where you can watch it. Make notes and sketches in your journal. How do the crystals form?

7. It takes time to grow large crystals, so be patient. When they get a little bigger, figure out a way to help them continue to grow on a string. Make notes and sketches in your journal on your procedure and the results.

8. When you think it's time, taste the crystals. Why is it called "rock candy"? Examine the crystals with your loupe, and compare them to your first drawings of sugar crystals. How are they alike? How are they different?

9. Here's a little challenge: Can you devise a way to grow one huge crystal on a string?

I WONDER...
Why do you suppose grown-ups worry when their water pipes freeze in the wintertime?

DID YOU KNOW?
Water, unlike other liquids, expands when it's frozen. The long, pyramid-shaped crystal structure of water traps space inside. How could you test this out?

INVESTIGATE SOME MORE!
Try growing crystals by varying the temperature or rate of cooling, or grow them on different objects—on a wooden Popsicle™ stick or straw for instance. Try growing salt crystals the same way. Simply change the sugar to salt. Keep careful records—do you use more or less salt?

EXPERIMENT 2: AMAZING CRYSTALS!

SUPPLIES
alum (found in the
  spices section of
  the grocery store)
goggles
saucepan
spoon
2 glass jars

Get ready to grow some spectacular crystals—**no strings attached**!

1. Put on your goggles and you're ready to roll. Pour about 1/2 cup of water into a pan, heat it over medium heat, and add alum until you have a supersaturated solution.

2. Let the solution cool and then carefully pour it into a jar. Keep your jeweler's loupe handy. What do you see in just a short period of time?

3. Pour off the solution into the other jar and pick out the biggest of these tiny crystals from the bottom of the first jar. (It's okay to use your fingers— just keep them away from your face and wash your hands when done.) Place these crystals in the new jar of solution. Discard the smaller crystals, rinse out the jar, and set it aside.

4. Check your crystals the next day. What changes do you see? Do the same thing as before: Transfer the solution carefully into the other jar, pick out the biggest crystals from the bottom of the first jar, and place them in the new jar of solution. Rinse out the other jar. Continue to do this every day until you are growing 3 or 4 crystals.

5. How do these crystals differ from the sugar crystals? Look at them through your loupe. What differences do you see? How big do you think they'll get?

6. Do you think you could convince two crystals to grow together? In a week or two, pick out two crystals with similar smooth faces and devise a method to test it out.

7. Write a fantasy story about what could happen as these crystals continue to get bigger and BIGGER! Hey, if they get big enough, you can probably charge your friends a quarter for a look!

INVESTIGATE SOME MORE!

· Boric acid and epsom salts, found in drugstores, also make lovely crystals. Start a batch of each and compare the results!

· Grow crystals from regular salt and sea salt and compare.

WARNING DO NOT MIX ANY OF THE ELEMENTS SUCH AS BORIC ACID, EPSOM SALTS, OR ALUM TOGETHER. WORK WITH EACH SUBSTANCE SEPARATELY.

EXPLORE SOME MORE

GOOD ENOUGH TO EAT!

Tell your mom and dad you're simply practicing science and cook yourself up a batch of yummy crystals in the form of fudge! (It's polite to share.)

Rocky Road Fudge

4 (4 1/2 oz.) milk chocolate bars
3 c. miniature marshmallows
3/4 c. broken nuts (walnuts, pecans, almonds, or filberts)

1. Break the chocolate in pieces and melt them in the top of a double boiler over hot (not boiling) water.

2. While the chocolate pieces are melting, grease an 8" x 8" x 2" pan with butter.

3. Remove the melted chocolate from the heat and beat it with a spoon until it's smooth. Stir in the marshmallows and nuts. Don't worry, it's supposed to be lumpy!

4. Spread the candy in the buttered pan and chill it in the refrigerator until firm. Cut it into squares.

"Good" fudge is creamy and velvety because the sugar crystals are very small. If the fudge is sugary and grainy, the sugar crystals are too large!

CRYSTAL CAVERNS

Generally, the forms in these limestone caverns are referred to as stone or rock. To grow them you make a supersaturated solution using washing soda.

SUPPLIES

goggles • measuring cup • tablespoon • food coloring • plate • 2 glass jars • washing soda • spoon • 3 pieces of fat wool yarn (each 30") braided together

WARNING DO NOT TASTE! IT WILL TASTE BAD AND THE SOLUTION IS CAUSTIC—IT WILL BURN YOUR THROAT.

All the experiments in this chapter start by making a supersaturated solution—this time using washing soda. Clear a space where the jars will not be bumped or moved.

1. Put on your goggles. Fill two glass jars half full of very hot water. Spoonful by spoonful, add washing soda to each of them until no more will dissolve. How many spoonfuls of washing soda do you need to add before the liquid is saturated? Note it in your journal.

 DID YOU KNOW?
No two snow crystals are alike, but they all have six sides and grow in either platelike or columnar patterns, depending on the air temperature and the amount of moisture.

2. Take the braided yarn. Put one end in each of the two jars so it droops down over a plate in between.

3. Think like a scientist. What do you predict will happen? Why? Make some notes in your journal. As your cavern begins to grow, experiment with food coloring for some real fun!

TAKE A TRIP!

Imagine seeing giant versions of the caverns you are growing! Water with lime from limestone rocks drips from the cave's ceiling. As the water goes into the air, it leaves behind the lime, which builds up over thousands of years. Here's an easy way to remember which is which: **Stalagmites** grow up from the **g**round; **stalactites** grow down from the **c**eiling and resemble giant icicles. Sometimes they meet and grow together! Read up on these caves in the library. Where in the U.S. could you go to see some of them?

FOR FURTHER EXPLORATION
Crystal and Gem by R.F. Symes and K.R. Harding (New York: Knopf, 1991).

BUBBLE UP!

Bubbles have always held a certain kind of magic for young and old alike. Ever seen little babies blow bubbles with saliva? Hey, I bet YOU did that! It's not necessary to understand the structure of bubbles to have fun with them, but since you're thinking scientifically, you might be interested in some bubble facts.

Cohesion and Surface Tension

Water molecules, like little magnets, are attracted to each other. They stick to each other, and not to air, through a force called **cohesion.**

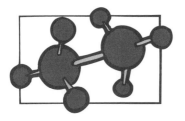

Because of **surface tension,** cohesion is strongest at the surface of water, because the water is pulled back into itself—down (into the water) and sideways (but not up, since in that direction there is only air).

Water can make bubbles all by itself, but soap makes bubbles last much longer. This is because soap decreases the surface tension. The pesky soap molecules muscle their way in between the water molecules and break up its hold, causing the molecules on the surface to s-t-r-e-t-c-h and form bigger, longer-lasting bubbles. The next time you do dishes, grab your bubble wand. Catch one and slowly blow air into it. Watch it gracefully lift off. Okay, enough science stuff. Now finish the dishes.

DID YOU KNOW?
It's true! The bubbles in your washing machine or bathtub are just for fun. They don't get you, or your socks, any cleaner. How would you explain this?

ENVIRONMENTAL ALERT!
Detergents that use phosphates end up in rivers and lakes. These phosphates cause algae to grow and suck the oxygen out of the water. The lack of oxygen causes fish and other wildlife to die, which in turn increases the pollution of the water. Make sure your family uses biodegradable soaps and detergents that have no phosphates.

See Chapter 6 in *Force, Of Course!* for more about the cohesive properties of water molecules.

EXPERIMENT 1: BUBBLEMANIA

Practically everyone knows how to blow bubbles. There's no special trick to it. But as a scientist, you can start testing some procedures and keeping track of the results in your journal. After that, you can get fancy. No telling what you'll create!

Start simple—with the bubble solution you can find in any store. Even professional bubble blowers swear by the plain old store-bought stuff. Mr. Bubbles® is one common brand that works well. Pour the solution into a plastic bowl, find an outdoor place with no wind, and then do what comes naturally!

1. Dip your bubble wand and a little of the handle into the solution, pucker up, and blow gently.

2. To close up your bubble while it's still on the wand, you have to close the opening you blew through by turning over the wand and sealing it. What happens to the air if you don't? (What else responds in the same way?)

3. Practice and see what works for you. REMEMBER! Keep the wand and some of the handle wet at all times.

Compare the results with a solution you make from a little dishwashing liquid (like Dawn®) and warm water. Some people also like to add a tiny bit of glycerin (maybe 1 tablespoon) to their homemade bubble brew. Try your homemade solution with and without glycerin.

Make a little chart in your journal to keep track of your results. What will you test for?

SUPPLIES
plastic bowl
warm water
store-bought bubble brew
    (like Mr. Bubbles®)
        OR
liquid dishwashing soap
    (like Dawn®)
1 tablespoon glycerin

Under what conditions will you test your bubbles? Involve a parent or other adult in your planning. Here are some possibilities:

- strongest bubbles?

- store-bought versus homemade solution?
- homemade solution with and without glycerin?
- homemade solution with warm and cold water?
- solution with sugar and gelatin added?

SUPPLIES 7

Mr. Bubbles® or home-
made bubble juice
bubble wand
straw

EXPERIMENT 2: BUBBLE-OMETRY

Ready to really get bold, to go where no bubble blower has ever gone before? Well, some have, and have even lived to tell about it.

Creepy Crawlies

Think you could make a whole string of little bubbles attached to each other? Sure you could. Here's how:

1. Blow a little bubble with your wand and then quick, catch it on the bottom of the wand so it's hanging down. Or, take your straw, blow a little bubble onto the bottom of the wand, and then quickly remove the straw. It takes a little practice, but no problem. You're a scientist. Gotta have patience. (**Hint:** Blow bubbles out of doors and out of the wind!)

2. Now use the straw to blow another bubble on the bottom of the first one. Always keep your straw wet by dipping it into the bubble liquid before touching the bottom bubble.

3. Keep adding to your creature by adding bubbles to the bottom bubble using your straw.

Find a partner and take turns sketching what you see. Use your loupe to see the structure of your creepy crawlie close up. Watch out though—they've been known to get kinda wild.

Picasso Special

Picasso was a very famous Cubist painter. Look at some of his paintings and you'll see why. In this experiment you'll create little cube shapes in the center of your bubbles. Are you ready for this? Do a few pushups and knee-bends to get yourself thoroughly warmed up.

1. Blow a bubble and use your straw to blow another bubble attached to the bottom of the first. See where they connect?

2. Blow a series of five or six little bubbles around that midpoint. Be sure and check out the angles, shapes, and corners. Have your friend sketch some of these patterns, or you sketch while your friend blows the bubbles for a change!

3. Now, find the place where all the bubbles meet in the center. Put your wet straw into that place and blow one last little bubble. What shape do you create?

4. Don't be discouraged if you can't do it the first few times. Just have fun, keep practicing, and observe the structures you do create. (Eventually you just may see a cube in the center!)

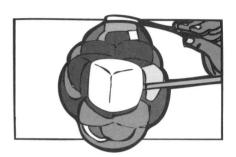

GRAVITY RULES

Quietly observe a bubble hanging down from your wand. The top of the bubble gets thinner and thinner and finally can no longer support the weight at the bottom. Guess what happens then? Why doesn't gravity pull the bubble to the ground immediately?

(**Hint:** Think about surface tension, and reread the introduction. Can you explain it in your own words in your journal?)

HUMONGOUS BUBBLES!

SUPPLIES:
plastic drinking straws,
    various shapes and widths
bucket
1/2 gallon* warm water
1/2 cup* dishwashing liquid
    (such as Dawn®)
1/2 T.* glycerin
    *[You can double these if
    you want]
lots of bubble wands (a loop of
    heavy cotton string, coat
    hanger bent into a big circle,
    piece of screen, little plastic
    fruit baskets, your hands!)

Head outside for these bubbles; they'll
make a major mess in the house! And
find a place with no wind. Wind adds
nothing to your bubble-blowing skills.

Mix yourself up some of this delightful
concoction in a big tub (big enough to
fit your bubble wand in it, up to and
including a little of the handle).
Practice swirling these beauties
gracefully off your wand with a twist of
your wrist. What is the difference
between these bubbles and the
smaller bubbles you made? You're
right, they're very oozy! Some of them
even seem to have personalities. (It's fine
to call them by name. No one will know.)

Observe them in the sunlight. Where
do their rainbow colors come from?
What do you see reflected in the bubbles?
Are all the images right side up?

Try making some bubbles between
your hands. Watch your
eyes, so no bubbles pop
in your face! Soap in the
eyes is NO FUN, as you
very well know.

BUBBLE EXTRAVAGANZA

Bubbles are as good an excuse as any
for a party! Get your friends to help
organize a Bubble Extravaganza some
warm and windless summer after-
noon. On the invitation (in the shape
of a bubble), ask everyone to bring
their own special bubble concoctions
and an assortment of bubble wands.

Hmm... any self-respecting party
needs food, right?—of COURSE! Serve
carbonated drinks (you know, the kind
with bubbles), popcorn, bubble gum
(Warning: Gum could interfere with
your bubble blowing), and later, when
everyone's ready to relax, show *The
Blob* or some other bubbly PG-rated
video. (We're sure you can think of
one.)

FOR FURTHER EXPLORATION
Molecules by Janice Van Cleave (New
    York: John Wiley, 1993).
Soap Science by J. Bell (Redding, MA:
    Addison-Wesley, 1993).

NO KIDDING!
A famous bubble blower in the
Pacific Northwest once blew a
bubble around two grown-up
people and then married them
inside the bubble! (He practiced for a very long time.)

DID YOU KNOW?
There are some people, adults
and children, who are born
without any immune system.
This means that the slightest
little germ could kill them.
These people live their whole
lives in specially designed
bubbles that protect them
from germs and diseases.

HOLD THE BUTTER, PLEASE!
Take a trip to a store that
wraps and ships packages and
see the kinds of plastic bubble
wrap and other protective
packing materials they use.
Why are so many of them
forms of bubbles? You may not
believe this, but one of the
best packing materials is plain
old popcorn! Why do you think
this is so?

IT'S ALL IN THE SEED

Seeds are independent critters. They carry within them everything they need to begin life. As soon as they push above the surface, they use the sun's energy (through a process called **photosynthesis**) to make food.

In the next two chapters we'll look at plants, including their stems and leaves. But let's start at the beginning, with seeds. They come in many colors, shapes, and sizes—all geared to support their unique methods of travel and to adapt to their environment and way of life. They are also very tough, designed not to break down until just the right conditions arise–pretty incredible when you think about it.

Seeds travel through **dispersal**. But why? What would happen if instead they all just fell directly to the ground from a tree or bush?

Think about the question in terms of people. Are there any basic needs that people and seeds share? Why did settlers move West?

Why do some families move from the city to the country? Why do people buy full-spectrum light bulbs? What are full-spectrum lights designed to do? What happens when people live in overcrowded conditions? Your answers might give you clues about what seeds need in order to survive and grow into strong, healthy plants.

Some seeds burst open, some blow in the wind, and others hang on tight while they're carried along by other living things. Some even resemble aircraft—take **samaras,** for example (some people call them whirligigs). What does their shape remind you of? How does their shape help them travel?

Use your journal to design and sketch your very own Super Seed, made for travel.

People and seeds share a basic need for light, space, and food. Seeds that travel increase their chances of finding good places to put down roots.

EXPERIMENT 1: GROWING ROOM

SUPPLIES
2 clear plastic glasses,
the same size
40 pea seeds
water

We all know that seeds need water to grow. But does water help them germinate faster?

What about soaking them in something besides water? Test it out for yourself in the next two experiments.

1. Take a moment to look closely at the seeds with your loupe. See how wrinkled they are. Why do you think this is? Think about the other seeds you may have collected. What do you think a pea's bumpy texture enables it to do?

2. To find out, draw one life-sized pea seed on a piece of paper. Then put 20 seeds in a glass of water to soak overnight. Put the other 20 seeds in the other plastic glass, but don't add any water.

3. Check them out the next morning—even before you brush your teeth. What happened? Is there any water left? How much difference is there between the two glasses?

4. Take out one of the wet seeds and draw it life-sized on the paper next to your first drawing and compare. How much did the seed swell overnight?

5. What does the wrinkled quality of some seeds allow them to do? Can you think of other objects that are designed in a similar way? Have you observed any other patterns, shapes, and textures that could help a seed?

SEED SCAFFOLDING
The designs on a seed are not just for looks. They help stabilize the seed's structure, just like the framework of a shell, building, or honeycomb does. How many different seed designs can you discover and draw in your journal?

BAGGY KNEES
If you've ever been lucky enough to see a newborn baby, you may have noticed all the baggy skin around those cute little knees and elbows! What do you think that baggy skin is for?

INVESTIGATE SOME MORE!

Use your softened seeds to make a structure using toothpicks as connectors. (You may want to soak more seeds.)

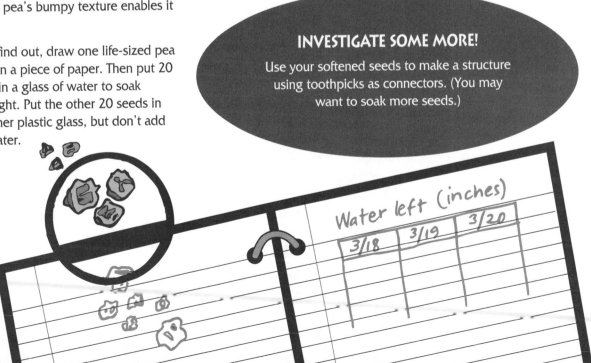

Water left (inches)

3/18	3/19	3/20

EXPERIMENT 2: SOAKING IT UP

SUPPLIES
18 bean seeds
3 glass jars
milk
3 paper cups
3 cups potting soil
pencil

How much difference does soaking make in **germination** time (the time it takes for a seed to develop roots, stems, and leaves)? And, soaking in what?

1. Count out 18 bean seeds, 6 in each jar. Cover 6 of them with water. Leave 6 dry.

2. My grandmother soaked her pea seeds in milk. She said the protein in the milk helped them grow—you know, just like it would help me if I'd drink my milk. Just for fun, take the last 6 seeds and soak them in a small glass of milk overnight. Do it for your grandmother. But no matter what you find, trust me. Her sweet peas were dynamite.

3. The next day, take 3 paper cups, carefully labeling each cup "WATER," "MILK," and "DRY."

4. Before adding the potting soil, carefully make 2 or 3 small pokes in the bottom of each cup for water drainage. Fill each cup about 3/4 full with potting soil and dampen it slightly.

5. To plant the seeds, make 6 little holes in the soil in each cup. To measure, push the eraser end of your pencil down to the end of the metal (about 3/4 inch), so you can plant all 18 seeds at exactly the same depth.

Cover the seeds with some potting soil, and water gently until a little water drains out the bottom. Set them on a tray (to catch the water) near a sunny window.

6. Which seeds do you think will germinate first? Write your prediction in your journal.

7. Water them the same amount as needed to keep the soil damp. Mark each cup's growth in your journal over the next week. Which plants pop through the soil first?

THE ACID TEST
Water isn't the only thing that helps soften a seed's tough covering. When animals eat seeds, their stomach acids and acids in the soil help soften the seeds.

SMART SEEDS
If your socks, stomach, dog, or bedroom floor had what seeds needed to grow, they'd all have vines, plants, fruits, and vegetables growing out of them. (Who would want to grow in YOUR socks, anyhow? Now you know how smart seeds are.) But if you want to draw a picture, go ahead!

DID YOU KNOW?
Some plants, like the Ponderosa pine, need fire to survive. Fire cleans out the area; then the seeds germinate.

INVESTIGATE SOME MORE!
Select 12 different kinds of seeds (flowers, fruits, and vegetables) and see which ones germinate the fastest. When would it be good to know this? Then step back, take a breath, and remember that it's not always necessary to be first.

EXPLORE SOME MORE

ADD SOME ZIP TO YOUR LIFE— WITH SPROUTS!

Did you know that bean sprouts—those cute little wiggly things—are very good for you? They are high in protein, and best of all, you can grow an unlimited supply right in your own kitchen. You can add sprouts to just about anything, including sandwiches, salads, and scrambled eggs. Yum! Here's how. You'll need some glass jars and some squares of cheesecloth.

Grab a combination of beans—it's more fun and flavorful to have a variety. Garbanzo, azuki, and lima beans are tried and true favorites.

1. Soak each variety overnight in a glass of water.

2. Pour out the water and rinse them. Place the beans in their own separate jars. Cover each jar with a piece of cheese-cloth and fasten it with a rubber band.

3. Each morning and evening, rinse the beans thoroughly. Between rinsings, keep the jar tilted at an angle in a dish rack, top down, so the water drains out through the cheesecloth. In about 3 days, you'll see white sprouts.

4. Sprouts are most nutritious when they are very short. After they've sprouted, keep them in the refrigerator to stop their growth. What are some common characteristics of all the sprouts that you have grown?

5. Happy grazing!

TRAVELIN' SHOES

Shuffle through a field sometime and check your clothes and hair when you get back home. What hitchhiked a ride home with you?

Scrutinize these seeds up close with your magnifying glass. Did you pick up any with little hooks, spines, or one-way arrows, like fishhooks?

Make a graph drawing of your body and plot your findings. What hooked where? Can you identify some patterns in these seeds' attachment sites?

AAH-CHOO!

If you live where people sneeze a lot in the springtime, you're in a perfect place to collect some pollen. Smear some glycerin on a glass slide. Leave it outside for a day or two and look at what you collected through your loupe and, if at all possible, through a microscope. How could you determine if different pollens are in the air at different times of the day?

MOVE OVER, HALLMARK

Create a whole series of drawings of magnified seeds and leaves, or create a crazy set (you know, with vines growing out of your socks). Turn them into notecards for a great present!

> **DID YOU KNOW?**
> Mother Nature's seed banks are in the ground where they lie dormant for over 10 years. Scientists keep seeds they collect in the refrigerator. Why? What does cold do to the seed?

> **FOR FURTHER EXPLORATION**
> *Seeds, Pop! Stick! Glide!* by Patricia Lauber (New York: Crown, 1991).

WHAT'S ON TOP?

After a seed germinates, things go every which way. Part of the new plant grows down into the soil in the form of roots that absorb water and needed minerals for the plant, while the shoot grows up in search of light.

When it pokes above the soil it turns green and can begin to make its own food, changing energy from the sun into food in a process called **photosynthesis.**

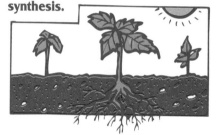

A plant's stems and leaves are major players in this important process.

Stems—More Than to Hang Leaves On

If you were going to custom-design a stem for a plant, what would be your main goal? Picture the "stems" of petunias and giant redwoods.

How do they differ? Why aren't they interchangeable? In both cases their stems are shaped like hollow tubes. What do you suppose the function is?

Leaves—Reach Out and Touch Someone

Some leaves resemble big flat hands that reach out and receive the energy from the sun needed for photosynthesis. How do leaves differ in dry, hot environments or in very cold, barren environments? Look at plants where

you live. How are leaves arranged on the stems to give the most access to light? How many different types of leaves can you find? Draw some stems and leaves in your journal that show variations on this light-loving scheme.

> A stem's hollow tube allows nutrients to be moved inside the plant. The stem must also be strong enough to support the plant's height.

DID YOU KNOW?

You can swing from the trees like you-know-who. Just find yourself a nice liana vine in a tropical forest. Their rope-like stems can wind around trees as tall as the Empire State Building and are strong enough to cheerfully hold up you, your friends—and a daredevil elephant.

EXPERIMENT 1: NATURE'S STRAWS

SUPPLIES
3 stalks of celery, with
 leaves attached
small knife
3 glass jars
salt
sugar
masking tape

General Sherman is a giant Sequoia tree and the world's largest living thing. Just how does water get up to the top of something that's over 275 feet high—moving against the force of gravity, no less? By **capillary action** and **transpiration.** See for yourself.

1. Snip a little off the bottom of each stalk of celery. Look at the ends with your loupe and do a drawing in your journal.

2. Put a cup of water in each glass. Add 2–3 spoonfuls of sugar to one glass and 2–3 spoonfuls of salt to the other. Stir each one until dissolved. The third glass is plain water. Label each glass SUGAR, SALT, and PLAIN with masking tape.

3. Place a stalk of celery in each glass. Leave them for 2 days. What do you think will happen?

4. Taste a leaf from each stalk. (**Note:** It's safe to taste sugar and salt. Scientists don't usually go around tasting experiments, unless of course they're cooking dinner.)

5. What happened and why? Record the results in your journal. Then, pass the celery at dinner and explain how plants get the nutrients they need.

6. Experiment with other flavorings such as lemon juice, or vanilla, peppermint, or chocolate extract. Do you think they will all behave like the salt and sugar? Why or why not?

7. Try this: Carefully make two vertical cuts up the stem of one celery stalk with leaves. Drape each strand in a different colored jar of water. Draw your prediction and the results. How else could you test capillary action?

JUST A QUESTION
Do you think your hair would turn rainbow-colored if you stood barefoot in colored water for two days? Why not? (Okay, go ahead and draw it, but PULEEASE, don't do it. Your toes will get all wrinkly.)

INVESTIGATE SOME MORE!
Snip 1/2 inch off the ends of three long-stemmed white carnations and flatten the ends with a hammer. Put 20–40 drops of a different food coloring in three small glasses and add a flower to each jar. What do you *predict* will happen? Check them the next day. Did each color work equally well? (Now you know how they get those silly lime green carnations for St. Patrick's Day.)

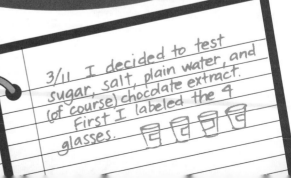

3/11 I decided to test sugar, salt, plain water, and (of course) chocolate extract. First I labeled the 4 glasses.

EXPERIMENT 2: LEAFY GREENS

SUPPLIES

- fresh beet or spinach leaves
- goggles
- small glass jar
- coffee filter
- sand
- rock & bowl, or mortar & pestle
- cotton swabs or flat toothpicks
- rubbing alcohol

In the fall, plants need to shed their leaves in order to hold water within themselves through the winter when water is frozen in the soil. In the process, plants also stop producing as much **chlorophyll,** the green pigment that makes leaves green. As the green fades, two other pigments can be seen, turning trees beautiful shades of yellow, orange, and red.

In this experiment you can discover some of these hidden leaf colors for yourself in a process known as **chromatography.**

1. Tear the leaves into small pieces and grind them in a bowl using a smooth rock. Add something gritty like a little sand (preferably white), and use a smooth rock or mortar and pestle to help crush the leaves.

2. Put on your goggles and carefully add a little rubbing alcohol. Continue grinding until it's turned into a dark green oozy liquid.

WARNING ! HAVE AN ADULT HELP YOU. DO NOT TASTE OR INHALE THE FUMES OF RUBBING ALCOHOL, AND KEEP IT AWAY FROM HEAT. IT IS FLAMMABLE.

3. Take a white coffee filter (they're already a nice cone shape), and using a cotton swab or flat toothpick, carefully paint (in 25–30 coats, letting it dry in between) some of the green liquid in a tiny little dot about 1 1/4 inches from the pointy end of the cone.

4. Carefully pour some rubbing alcohol into a clear glass jar (with adult help) and submerge the cone so the bottom 1/2 inch touches the alcohol but NOT the green dot. Tape the top of the cone to the jar if necessary to keep it from falling too far into the jar, and screw on the cap. What do you think will happen?

5. Remove the cone from the jar and unfold it in about 10 minutes. What do you see? What do you think happened to cause this?

DID YOU KNOW?
Besides making the air breathable for all living things, leaves are also used in teas, dyes, medicines, chewing gum, car wax, and baskets. What leaves do we eat? List more examples in your journal and make a poster, honoring our friends, the leaves.

TAKE A SNOOZE ON A WATER LILY
The Royal water lily is the world's biggest water plant. It has giant floating leaves several feet in diameter. Each leaf has a 3–4 inch edge that prevents it from curling up. Imagine—a small child could float on one!

INVESTIGATE SOME MORE!
What other plants, birds, and fruits contain the same bright red, yellow, and orange pigments as fall leaves? Make a drawing or collage that celebrates these colors in nature.

EXPLORE SOME MORE

LEAF SKELETONS

Leaves with all the green tissue removed are called **leaf skeletons**. You may spot some of these lacy leaf skeletons ready-made in a local park, but if not, here is a way to re-create the process over several months.

1. Snag some big, roundish, green leaves on the ground in your neighborhood.

2. Put them in a jar of water in a dark, warm place in your house. Yum, yum! Almost immediately, little organisms start munching on these tender leaf morsels. (**Note:** Be warned! Don't choose your closet for this experment! The jar will begin to smell as the leaves rot.)

3. Add water as needed to keep the leaves underwater.

4. In 2 or 3 months, carefully spring a leaf from the jar. Place it on a glass plate. Carefully remove all the rotted tissue with a cotton-swab or a tiny paintbrush. Lift off the skeleton that's left and rinse it in a pan of water. Dry it between pieces of construction paper or blotting paper, and then finish the drying by pressing it between several sheets of newspaper, weighted under something heavy.

5. Look at this delicate skeleton under your loupe. Write your impressions in the form of a poem in your journal.

If you have several leaf skeletons, mount them on construction paper as cards for special friends, or frame them as works of art—compliments of you and Mother Nature.

6. Don't forget to wash all your supplies and generally clean up. It's all a part of doing science.

LEAFY LETTERS

Collect some small leaves, weeds, and flowers that have fallen in your yard (it's important to always ask if it's okay).

Dry, press, and mount them on folded pieces of construction paper to make a beautiful set of notecards.

BIG IDEAS

Visit a greenhouse, arboretum, or old-growth forest and b-r-e-a-t-h-e! The oxygen and the moist coolness from the plants' transpiration process make them wonderful places to spend time. Contrast this with a trip to a rock or cactus garden—environments with very different leaf structures.

How does full leaf structure versus reduced leaf structure change the environment? How does each environment make you *feel*? Compare and contrast these in your journal in the form of drawings, impressions, and poems.

FOR FURTHER EXPLORATION
Miss Rumphius by Barbara Cooney (New York: Viking Penguin, 1982).
Linnea in Monet's Garden by Christina Bjork (New York: Farrar, Straus &Giroux, 1987).

WHO CAN I LIVE ON?

Think you're "home alone"? Not on your life! At this very moment you're breathing, eating, walking on, and generally cozying up to moldy microlife in every part of your day. And what makes up this community we often forget (until we clean out the refrigerator, that is)? Molds, fungi, lichens—neat stuff like that.

Fungi live everywhere—in the air, in the water, and in the soil. True fungi (including mushrooms, molds, and mildew) have one thing in common: they all lack chlorophyll, the green pigment that other plants use to make food. Because they can't make their own food, they have to form partnerships to get what they need to survive. They do this by getting food from the plants and animals they live on or from feeding on decaying matter (like that tasty donut you so kindly left in the lunch sack in your locker at least two months ago).

Still other fungi such as yellow and orange lichens found on rocks and trees in the forest are the result of a partnership between algae and fungi. The fungi gets the food it needs from algae and provides the algae a nice damp home.

Look at it this way. You've lived this long. You might as well take a deep breath, get up all your courage, and plunge deeper into the awesome world of fungi and molds.

Fungi need air, water, and food—just like you!

ORGANIC DIAPERS
In the olden days parents used moss for diapers. The fact is, sphagnum moss can hold a whopping 27 times its weight in water! Why would a plant be able to do this? Why do you think this moss was used for bandages during World War I?

THINK BIG—CHECKS AND BALANCES
Some mushrooms are poisonous. Some populations of animals threaten other species of animals. Fires destroy acres of natural habitat. How do these structures and events provide built-in checks and balances in our world?

For more about who gets the leftovers, see *Close Encounters!*, Chapter 10.

EXPERIMENT 1: MOLDY OLDIES

Molds may appear on foods by accident, but in this experiment you are going to scientifically grow molds—on purpose.

1. Snag a moldy piece of bread from that old lunch sack in your locker, or grow your own by sprinkling a little water on a slice of bread and leaving it in a loosely tied plastic bag in a warm, dark place for several days.

2. When a nice crop of mold appears, take out the bread. Observe it under your loupe and draw a picture of it in your journal. You will use this mold to "seed" mold growth on other foods.

3. Take a toothpick (or cotton swab) and carefully scrape some of the mold off one part of the bread. Wipe it on a section of a piece of fruit or vegetable until you can see it. Throw away that toothpick and, using a new one each time, gather mold from a different part of the bread and paint it on each item.

4. Place each sample in its own container and sprinkle each one with about 2 tablespoons of water.

5. Loosely close each bag or container and place them in a cardboard box with a lid.

6. Check the jars after 3 or 4 days and record the results. Did more mold grow on some samples than others? Is all the mold the same color as the bread mold? If not, what caused the different colors?

DID YOU KNOW?
The green mold seen on oranges is **penicillium.** One penicillium mold is used to make penicillin, an important antibiotic that your doctor may prescribe when you're sick.

SUPPLIES
fruits and vegetables (orange, strawberry, lemon, tomato, small piece of broccoli, sweet potato, or carrot)
one slice of bread
measuring spoon
plastic bags with twist ties, small plastic containers, or small glass jars (one for item above)
toothpicks (or cotton swabs)
rubber bands and small pieces of cloth to cover containers (if needed)

AN APPLE A DAY MAY KEEP THE DOCTOR AWAY BUT MOLDY ORANGES CAN HELP YOU GET WELL, TOO!

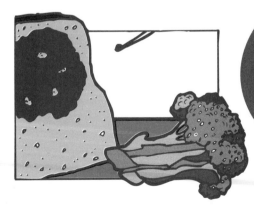

INVESTIGATE SOME MORE!

· Try growing molds on the same item (a) in the dark and light, (b) with and without water, and (c) with and without sugar. What do the results suggest to you about mold growth? What ideas would you like to explore further?

· Take three pieces of bread. For the first slice, follow the experimental procedure above. Wipe the second slice on the kitchen floor, and run the third slice across your forehead. Then follow the steps listed above. Label each container and make sure they all have the same growing conditions. Are all the molds the same?

EXPERIMENT 2: A FUNGUS AMONGUS

SUPPLIES
- a 5- or 10-gallon jar—the bigger the better, OR an old fish tank
- 5-6 damp, rotting leaves from a nearby park or trail
- 4-5 small pieces of rotting wood (damp, dark pieces about the size of your hand)
- 1 toothpick

Try an experiment with the molds that grow on wet leaves and twigs—slime molds! Look at slime molds under a powerful microscope. They may be oval or round, different colors, and usually grow on little stalks that look like stems. Most amazing of all, they can move. See for yourself!

1. Make a home for these molds that are just like the ones they love in woods and parks. Place several layers of construction paper or paper towels on the bottom of your jar or fish tank.

2. Place leaves and wood on the wet paper and cover the jar with cloth. Keep it moist for 2-3 weeks.

3. Don't move the jar. What do you see growing? Do you see any slimy, fingerlike molds? What color are they? Keep daily notes in your journal.

4. See if the mold will move. Pick one and stick a toothpick close to it to mark the place. Draw the mold in relation to the toothpick in your journal. Check back in a couple of hours. Where is the slime now? Observe it with your loupe.

SLIME MOLD
A 300-pound slime mold was found on a tree in Washington in 1946. Another newly discovered fungus, also in Washington, is listed in the *Guinness Book of World Records*. It covers 1500 square miles underground.

STRANGE BUT TRUE
You may think Camembert cheese smells like stinky gym socks, but some people pay BIG money for cheeses with green molds growing on them.

MUSHROOM HUNTING
Many people go mushroom hunting in the woods, but it can be dangerous. Every year people die from accidentally picking and eating highly poisonous wild mushrooms. Find a local expert to lead you on a safe mushroom walk. By the way, can you think of any advantages to being poisonous to some organisms?

5/11
Experiment: Growing slime molds

Description:

What I predict:

Results:
Day 1 -
Day 2 -

EXPLORE SOME MORE

MUSHROOM AND CHEESE SCRAMBLE

A tasty breakfast treat for your family, starring mushrooms—a famous fungi!

    3-4 eggs, beaten
    1 green onion, chopped in tiny pieces
    6-8 store-bought mushrooms,
        washed and thinly sliced
    1-2 tablespoons butter
    1/2 cup grated cheese
    frying pan

1. Beat the eggs in a bowl with a fork or egg beater. Set aside.

2. Put the butter in the frying pan on low heat. Add the mushrooms and green onion and gently cook, stirring often, for about 5 minutes.

3. Add the eggs, turn the heat up just a little, and cook, stirring constantly. When the eggs are almost done, add the cheese and continue stirring until the cheese melts.

4. Serve 'em up with whole wheat toast and juice for a special Sunday breakfast surprise.

MAKE SPORE PRINTS

1. Find a grocery store where you can buy several kinds of big mushrooms (one each) that are **open** on the bottom.

2. Carefully cut off the entire stem and place the mushroom cut-side-down on a sheet of paper. Cover it with a glass or bowl and let it sit for 2-3 hours. (Experiment with both black and white construction paper. White spore prints look neat against dark paper.)

3. Mushrooms will continue to drop spores and make prints for several days; move them around on the paper. Each variety of mushroom has its own unique spore color and pattern. In fact, color is a clue when identifying mushrooms in the wild.

4. If you end up with some great prints, use spray art fixative to adhere the spores to the paper and turn them into notecards.

THE LANGUAGE OF SLIME

We talk about "yucky" stuff or "slimy" characters. Why is this? Can you think of other ways our language devalues molds and slime—our champion recyclers and decomposers? How do molds and fungi fit into the structure of living things?

In our culture, how do we value (or devalue) people who have similar jobs? How could you help raise the consciousness and respect for the **people** who dispose of waste in restaurants or hospitals, collect trash, or buy and sell junk? What would happen if these jobs did not exist?

> **FOR FURTHER EXPLORATION**
> *Mushroom in the Rain* by Mirra Ginsburg (New York: Macmillan, 1990).

MAKE NO BONES ABOUT IT

"Make no bones about it" is an old saying that means to tell it like it is. It's a good place to start on most any subject—including bones and skeletons.

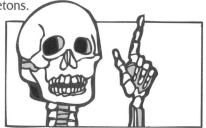

Animals with bones are called **vertebrates.** Vertebrates have been around for about 450 million years. All the bones that make up the frame of an animal or human are called a **skeleton.** Our skeleton gives us our shape and form, helps protect our vital organs, and, together with the muscles, enables our body to move.

Think about:
- the hind legs of a kangaroo
- the long legs of a great blue heron
- the skull of an elephant fish
- the skull of a woodpecker

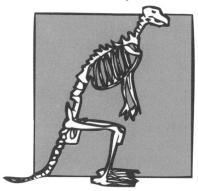

Which one is built for wading in deep water? hopping fast? pounding on wood? snagging food in small underwater crevices? Can you think of other animals, birds, and plants whose skeletal structures have specific purposes? How are they alike? How are they different? List and sketch them in your journal.

Human Skeleton

When you think about it, a rib cage looks a little like a catcher's mask. What is the purpose of a catcher's mask? What do you suppose your rib cage protects? What about your skull? What does it protect?

Have you ever felt the soft spot on a newborn baby's head? When you were born, your bones were soft and made of **cartilage.** As you grew, your bones began to harden; they were coated with calcium phosphate, supplied mainly from milk. This layer of calcium eventually seals all the bones, making more growth impossible. (Did you know your collarbone is still growing? It usually seals around age 20 to 25.)

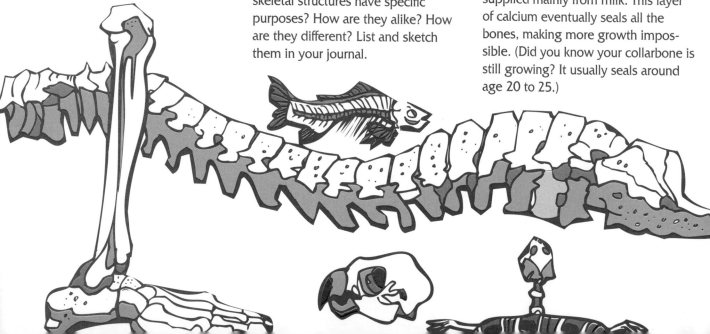

EXPERIMENT 1: WEAK IN THE KNEES

Our bones help us to balance, to walk upright, and to support our weight. For bones to be strong enough to do this important job, they need calcium, which we get from dairy products, sardines, salmon, collard greens, broccoli, and spinach. Active, weight-bearing exercise such as walking and running helps calcium stay in the bones so they remain strong and healthy.

Find out what happens to bones when they do not have enough calcium and are reduced to cartilage.

1. Broil or roast the chicken legs for a nice supper. What changes in the structure occur to the meat for our eating pleasure?

2. Carefully scrape any remaining meat off the chicken bones. Wash them in hot, soapy water and rinse and dry them. Weigh the bones. Are they hard or soft?

3. Put on your goggles and fill a glass jar with vinegar (enough to cover the bones). Screw on the cap and let the jar sit for two whole weeks. (Sometimes scientists must be very patient.) What do you think will happen?

4. At the end of two weeks, take out the bones and rinse them off in the sink. (If there has been no change, put them back in the vinegar solution for another week or more, and then test again.) What did the vinegar do to the calcium in the bones?

5. Dry them off and weigh them again. Is there a difference? Chart or draw any differences you observe.

6. Now for the fun part! What can you do with rubber bones? Tie them in a knot or a bow if you dare! Write or draw the results in your journal.

IF I HAD A BUNCH, BET I COULD MAKE A RUBBER CHICKEN!

7. Take a moment and think about what you learned from this experiment. Then drink your milk (or eat your yogurt).

INVESTIGATE SOME MORE!

· Try the same experiment with an egg. Leave it in the vinegar for about one week. What happened to the eggshell?

· Do you think other kitchen acids such as lemon juice or tomato juice would have the same results? Test them and see.

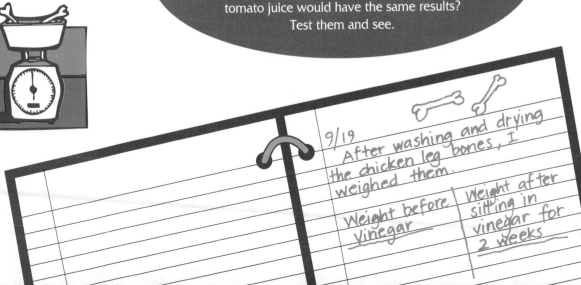

9/19
After washing and drying the chicken leg bones, I weighed them.

Weight before vinegar	Weight after sitting in vinegar for 2 weeks

EXPERIMENT 2: LEND A HELPING HAND

SUPPLIES
3 paper towel tubes
scissors
small screwdriver
tape
recycled produce twist
   tics
2 long, skinny balloons
string

Bones are nice, but alone they can't do much besides scare little kids on Halloween. Thanks to the teamwork of our bones and muscles, we can bend, lift, stretch, twist, run, hop, and jump.

Want to see how the muscles and bones work together in your arm? Use paper tubes to represent the bones (the humerus, ulna, and radius), and balloons to represent muscles (your biceps and triceps).

1. Cut the tubes to match the length of your arm as shown. Carefully cut each tube lengthwise and roll it into a smaller, more compact tube. Tape the seam of each tube.

2. Label each tube as shown.

3. Carefully poke a small hole through one end of each tube as shown. Run the twist tie through the six holes and twist the ends to hold it in place.

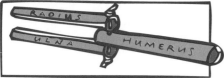

4. Test to see that the middle bone (the humerus) can move easily between the ulna and the radius.

5. Ready to attach the muscles? Loosely blow up both balloons and tie the ends.

6. The first balloon represents your biceps. Tie both ends onto the bones as shown with string. Then attach the second balloon to represent your triceps.

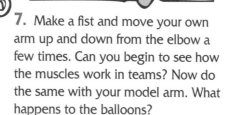

7. Make a fist and move your own arm up and down from the elbow a few times. Can you begin to see how the muscles work in teams? Now do the same with your model arm. What happens to the balloons?

8. Paint your model arm in the most colorful, artistic way you can. Attach a glove to the end, and give a friend a helping hand (with the glove holding flowers or a card!). You could also watch your real muscles work as you weed your grandma's garden.

DESIGNER ARM
Look at a picture of the mechanical arm on the U.S. space shuttle. See how the joints in this high-tech arm allow it to bend, twist, swivel, reach, and pick up heavy loads—very much like your own arm.

Why do you suppose it was designed this way? What does this suggest about the versatility of your own arm? Does the mechanical arm improve upon the original design model in any way?

FUNNY BONES
Ow! The pain you feel when you bump your elbow is not really coming from the bone—it's from your ulnar nerve, which is wedged close to the bone. What do you think is the function of this nerve?

STOP ME IF
YOU'VE HEARD
THIS ONE...

EXPLORE SOME MORE

SCRUMPTIOUS STRAWBERRY SMOOTHIE

This high-energy smoothie is full of calcium from milk and yogurt. Your bones will love you!

    1 cup milk
    1/2 cup lemon or vanilla yogurt
    5 or 6 frozen strawberries
    1/2 banana
    2 or 3 ice cubes, in pieces

Put all ingredients in a blender and buzz for about 30 seconds until thick and frothy. Pour into a tall glass and enjoy! But beware: You may become the Official Smoothie Maker for your family.

BONE ART

Many artists have drawn, painted, and sculpted skeletal structures and bones—or shapes that resemble bones. For starters, look at the work of David Smith, Leonardo da Vinci, Henry Moore, Fernand Léger, and Michelangelo. Then create some bone art of your own. Start by sketching a drumstick. Then mold some modeling clay into a bone shape, let it dry, and paint it (or create a mobile from lots of little bone shapes). You can also try your hand at doing some pencil drawings of hands and feet in as much detail as possible.

A LITTLE CONTEST

Idioms are expressions that, when looked at word by word, do NOT carry the literal meaning of the phrase! Many idioms are associated with parts of the body. For example:

    "Keep your nose out of my business!"
    "Gimme some elbow room!"
    "He's weak in the knees."
    "She gave him a knuckle sandwich."
    "Keep your eye on the ball!"

Get a big sheet of paper and post it in the kitchen so the whole family can take part. See if together you can list 10 idioms—especially those that pertain to parts of the body (extra credit if they pertain in some way to bones). Too easy? Try for 20 or even 30! You'll begin to identify them in conversations, books, TV, and movies. For added fun, pick your favorites to illustrate—literally, of course! And then give your bones a rest.

"KEEP YOUR EYE ON THE BALL"

BECOME AN ARCHAEOLOGIST

Archaeologists are true science detectives, piecing together information about life in earlier times from clues—often bones and fragments of bones and teeth—that they unearth. Interview an archaeologist and learn more about his or her work. Did you know that some organizations like Earthwatch give people 16 years of age and older a chance to visit parts of the world and become volunteer members of archaeological research teams?

DID YOU KNOW?

In the olden days, bones were used to make jewelry, tools, buttons, and dice.

Why were bones chosen to make certain objects? How do their structures make them good choices? Are bones still used to make these objects today? Why or why not?

FOR FURTHER EXPLORATION

The Skeleton and Movement by Steve Parker (New York: Franklin Watts, 1989).
Skeletons: An Inside Look at Animals by Jinny Johnson (Pleasantville, NY: Reader's Digest, 1994).

RUN FOR COVER!

People, birds, reptiles, mammals, and fish have bony internal skeletons called an **endoskeleton.** An endoskeleton includes a spine that helps support the body, and a rib cage and skull that protect the organs they enclose. This kind of skeleton can more easily accommodate a growing body.

Most animals, however, wear their bones on the outside. Called **exoskeletons,** these hard coverings often resemble a suit of armor. Exoskeletons also provide protection and support, but they have one big disadvantage. What do you suppose it is?

Did you know that tortoises and turtles are unique in their structure? Because they have a backbone and ribs attached to their outer shell, they are the only animals with both an endoskeleton and exoskeleton.

In this chapter you'll have a chance to examine several **mollusks,** the largest group of shelled invertebrates. They include most of what you think of as seashells, but also include crabs, oysters, clams, and even some shelled creatures that live on land (like the snail or slug that leaves a slimy trail in your garden).

You'll also have a chance to think wildly and creatively about the idea of "shells" and what they protect. Get ready, and let's explore!

GROWING ROOM

Do you know what a newborn turtle and human baby have in common? Both skeletal structures leave g-r-o-w-i-n-g room. Just like the sections of a newborn baby's skull aren't connected at birth, the bones of a newborn turtle's shell aren't yet fused together when it hatches.

THINK LIKE A SCIENTIST

Some turtles and crabs have soft shells. Can you think of any advantages to having a soft shell? What are the disadvantages?

HARD SHELL
VS.
SOFT SHELL

Because an exoskeleton can't expand as the body inside gets bigger, insects, shellfish, or other **invertebrates** (animals without a backbone) must shed their protective shell, add on to their existing shell, or grow a new one every so often.

EXPERIMENT 1: WHAT'S INSIDE?

It's fun to examine the inside of shells. Perhaps you have a shell collection and can donate a few different varieties to examine in the interest of science. Remember that it is up to us to protect these creatures. Don't ever remove anything from the beach that is alive—or inhabited! (For one thing, they smell!)

1. Lay down a sheet of newspaper on a table.

2. Put your sandpaper, grainy side up, on the newspaper. Take one shell at a time and carefully rub it back and forth on the sandpaper, slowly sanding away layers of the shell.

3. As you sand away layers, pick up

the shell every so often and see what you have uncovered. Examine it closely using your loupe or magnifying glass. Sharpen your powers of observation: Are there any hidden chambers that you didn't know existed before? Look for lines that were created as the shell grew. Can you see a pattern or regularity of growth lines? Are some parts more bumpy than others? What about the thickness/thinness? These are all clues about the life and time of that shell. Record and draw your observations.

4. Take a few moments to think about the creature that might have inhabited that shell. Sketch the shell and write a poem about it in your journal.

5. How does each shell differ? Did you find any similarities?

A HARD DAY'S NIGHT
Crabs are safe inside their shells, but because their shells don't grow, they must break out of them and grow new ones. Their new shell is very soft and takes several days to harden. During this time they have to hide from predators that might eat them.

VACANT HOUSE FOR RENT
Pieces of coral you can find on some beaches are really the structures of what were once living, growing colonies of tiny animals. Many coral reefs are older than humans on this earth, and are endangered due to collectors and pollution. Look at some coral with your jeweler's loupe and imagine all the animals that once inhabited all those little holes!

INVESTIGATE SOME MORE!
Examine the cross section of a chambered nautilus. The animal lives only in the outermost compartment of the shell, sealing off earlier sections as it grows. What happens to these sealed chambers? What is their purpose? Look at the size of each spiral. Where is a spiral always the biggest? smallest? Use your thinking skills to figure out: How does this shell's spiral shape accommodate the growing animal that lives inside?

SUPPLIES
white butcher paper
thick marking pens
tape

27

EXPERIMENT 2: A SHELL—FOR WHAT?

Now you will have a chance to think creatively about the protective nature of shells. This is a fun activity for the whole family.

1. To begin, divide your paper into four sections labeled: Object, Shell, What Does It Protect?, How Well Does It Do Its Job?

2. Challenge yourself and your family to list as many different "shells" as possible. Let's start with an easy one. How about eggshells? Too easy? Okay, what about nuts or seeds? Now really let your mind go: What protective shells are an everyday part of your life and you never, ever thought about them as "shells" until now?

Take your TV cabinet, for example. What is it made of? *wood? plastic?* What does it protect? *the fragile tubes from being bumped or broken? dust?* How well has this protective shell done its job? *Hint: Is your TV in one piece?*

You will be surprised how many protective shells you will begin to identify in the next week or two. Look for them in the grocery store, at school, at baseball practice, in the mall. Look high, look low. Be an investigator! Everywhere you go you'll see more to add to your list. What about outdoor music shells like the Hollywood Bowl?

3. Think about the material each shell is made of and what each one is uniquely designed to protect or enhance. Could you improve upon the design of any of these shells? How? Make some notes in your journal about one protective shell you feel certain you could improve upon. Then write to the company and make your idea known.

FOR INVENTORS ONLY!
Now that you have identified an amazing number of protective "shells," it's time to design one that does not yet exist.
- What would it do?
- Why would it be important?
- Who would use it?

Draw it in your journal and include a short description.

1/26

This is my "bed shell" with stereo speakers by my pillow and a TV at the foot of the bed.

EXPLORE SOME MORE

PATTERNS IN NATURE

Let your loupe take you for a walk in the world. See everything through its eyes. Look for patterns, up close and far away. Watch for patterns that you saw earlier in the shells you observed.

Take your choice! You can photograph them, draw them, make a collage of them, write poetry about them, and add them to your journal.

SPIRALS

We already identified the chambered nautilus shell. How about sunflowers, the horns of bighorn sheep, and spiral staircases? What other spirals can you think of? What purpose does a spiral shape serve?

EXPLOSIONS

There are inkspots and dandelions. What other explosion patterns can you identify?

POWER OF FIVE

This is a fun one! Look carefully at a sea urchin, sea star, and sand dollar. How many patterns of five can you identify? What other "five" patterns can you think of? Can you identify other number patterns (three, for instance)?

OTHER PATTERNS

What about the patterns on tortoise shells? Refer back to the sketches of bubbles you did in Chapter 2.

Do you see any similarities between the two? Can you think of anything else with this pattern?

What other patterns can you identify in nature and in architecture? Are patterns for visual interest? Why do patterns form in shells and seeds? What are the advantages and disadvantages?

NESTING INSTINCTS

Congratulations! As a new architect, you've been given the job of building a model of a bird's nest, another kind of shell when you stop to think about it. Nothing to it, you say? Try it! You'll have lots more respect for the architectural ability of birds.

1. Grab a friend and go on a scavenger hunt for nesting materials, perhaps grass, leaves, twigs, bark, feathers, dryer lint, pieces of string, torn bits of newspaper, and pieces of cloth. When you have a nice bag full, spread out your treasures and begin by tearing up everything you've gathered into tiny pieces. (Pause for a moment to consider that birds do all this without the use of two hands that include thumbs.)

2. Figure out a way to form these materials into a nest the way a bird does. (Sorry, birds don't use tape, glue, or chewing gum.) You could try making a long oriole's nest, like a sock, that hangs from a tree branch, or you could try making a nest that balances in the branches of a tree.

3. Write up your process in your journal. What materials were easiest to work with? What was the most difficult part?

MIRRORS

Many computers have drawing programs that include a "mirrors" function. This function lets you draw a pattern while the computer creates the mirror image. Have fun drawing some patterns and printing them out in black and white or in color. They can become designs for cards, posters, or even T-shirts! Then draw in a mirror and compare experiences.

L-O-N-GSTOCKINGS The long, stocking-shaped eggs of the Montezuma oropenola, a bird found in Mexico and Central America, can be 6 1/2 feet long!

IF I HAD TO LAY AN EGG THAT BIG I'D NEVER GET OFF THE NEST!

FOR FURTHER EXPLORATION
Shell by Alex Arthur (New York: Knopf, 1989).
Bimwili and the Zimwi by Verna Aardema (New York: Dial, 1985).

UP, UP, AND AWAY

Have you ever imagined what it would be like to be a bird? Close your eyes and picture yourself soaring, diving, and floating gracefully on the wind. How would things look from the air? Try drawing a "bird's-eye view" of the ground below.

Flying High

With birds, their feathers are the key. They're strong, light, and flexible. Damaged ones are easily replaced; in fact, birds replace most of their feathers at least once a year. Feathers streamline the body and provide insulation from the cold.

Collect some discarded feathers. You can tell where they came from by their shape.

Wing feathers, for example, are stiff, with no down. Notice their curve, and how one side is shorter than the other. *Body feathers* are often brightly colored with soft downy feathers on the end. What do you suppose the down is for? *Tail feathers* have more squarelike ends. They act like the rudder on a boat or plane, helping birds to balance and to steer when in flight.

For centuries, people have dreamed about flying. In this chapter we'll investigate flight. What is it that enables birds or planes to fly? What design is necessary for flight as opposed to walking, swimming, or skipping? What features are shared by things that fly (including the pollen you examined in Chapter 3)?

A LITTLE MYSTERY TO SOLVE
Why can bumblebees fly? Do some research, some scientific thinking, and then write an explanation in your journal.

Find out about thrust, lift, and drag in *Force, Of Course!,* Chapter 8.

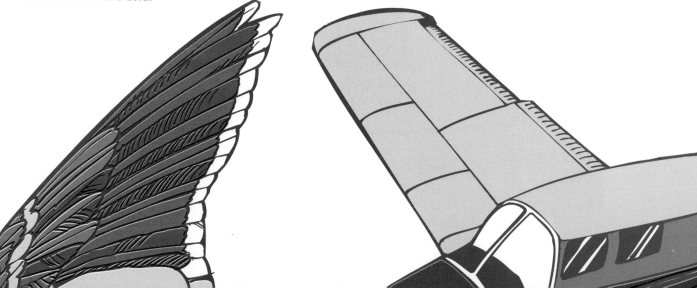

EXPERIMENT 1: DELIGHTFUL KITES

SUPPLIES

newspaper
large heavy plastic leaf
  bag
2 1/8 inch dowels, each
  about 6 1/2 inches long
2 1/8 inch dowels, each
  about 23 inches long
black electrical tape
a ball of string
scraps of colorful fabric
scissors
stickers and labels

Notice that kites have different forms of "backbones" and struts, very much like a bird. These dowels act as support for the thin, light structure.

The next time someone tells you to "go fly a kite," just say okay! Take a lesson from the birds and construct a kite.

1. Make the kite pattern out of a folded sheet of newspaper as shown and cut it out.

2. Put the newspaper pattern on top of the plastic bag. Place the long edge of the pattern along one side of the plastic bag with the opening at the bottom.

3. Cut the plastic around the newspaper, leaving the folded edge UNCUT, and unfold your kite.

BAG OPENING

4. Notice the rectangle shape on the inside of the kite. Tape the two LONG dowels on the vertical sides of the rectangle and the two SHORT dowels on the two outer sides of the kite with black tape as shown.

5. Make an anchor line by tying a piece of string about 36 inches long from one short dowel to the other. Leave the anchor line fairly loose. (You will want to experiment with the tightness of the anchor line.)

6. Tie a ball of string to the center of the anchor line.

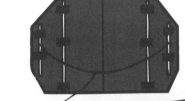

7. Make a tail by cutting little strips of fabric about 2 inches wide and 6 inches long. Tie them securely on a string about 2 feet long. (**Hint:** Tying the LINE to the BOWS keeps them from sliding.) Attach the tail to the kite as shown.

8. Decorate your kite with stickers and labels and then test it out! Think scientifically. Don't hesitate to make adjustments as necessary to improve your kite's performance.

INVESTIGATE SOME MORE!

• Imagine you are an inventor. What questions might you have in watching a kite? What might you discover? Make some field notes in your journal.

• Make yourself a pocket kite. Change the dimensions and make a small kite to carry around or to decorate your room.

EXPERIMENT 2: THE SKY'S THE LIMIT!

How is it that birds can fly and even glide in the air for hours? Put on your best thinking hat. Then dazzle your family with the scientific explanation:

The curved nature of birds' feathers and wings help produce **lift.** Here's how it works:

Cup your hand a little to make a curve with your palm down. See how the top of your hand is more curved than the underneath part? The air always moves faster over a curved top surface, and *faster moving air always means lower air pressure.*

Since a bird's wings are curved in the same way, the air pressure on the top of the wings decreases, while the pressure underneath remains the same. Because high-pressure air always moves toward a low-pressure area, the high-pressure air underneath the bird pushes up, producing lift.

This is called **Bernoulli's principle.** This principle also explains how an airplane can stay in the air and how your favorite pitcher can throw that mean curve ball!

You can see Bernoulli's principle at work in the simple experiment below. Then go out and practice your curve ball. You can name it the Bernoulli Blaster.

1. Take a sheet of plain notebook paper and cut a 1 1/2-inch strip off the bottom.

2. Place the paper against your bottom lip and blow across the top of the paper.

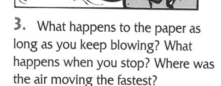

3. What happens to the paper as long as you keep blowing? What happens when you stop? Where was the air moving the fastest?

4. Think about Bernoulli's principle again. How does the paper act like the wing of a bird or an airplane?

5. Now think about how a pitcher makes a curve ball spin. Can you explain Bernoulli's principle at work? Draw a diagram first and then explain it in your own words in your journal.

DID YOU KNOW?
Some bird bones are hollow and some are actually filled with air. A passageway connecting the humerus bones directly to the lungs allows air from the lungs to flow directly into those bones to give the bird extra lift.

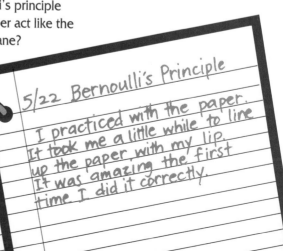

5/22 Bernoulli's Principle
I practiced with the paper. It took me a little while to line up the paper with my lip. It was amazing the first time I did it correctly.

EXPLORE SOME MORE

DON'T TRY THIS AT HOME!

Have you heard the Greek myth about Daedalus and Icarus, his young son, who are imprisoned in a tower by King Minos?

Daedalus, who is an inventor, plans their escape—by flying! Daedalus and his son fashion bird feathers into large wings and sew them together, using wax to curve them into winglike shapes.

Soon they're ready to begin their flying lessons. Icarus loves flying so much that he does not listen to his father's stern warnings. Each day he flies nearer and nearer the sun. What do you think happened?

To find out, get a copy of this exciting myth from your school or neighbor-hood library. There are many versions to choose from. One good one is *The Macmillan Book of Greek Gods and Heroes* by Alice Low (New York: Macmillan, 1985).

OWL PELLETS

Owls don't have teeth, so they swallow their prey whole. Their bodies digest the soft parts of the mouse, for example, and form the bones and fur into tight balls that they cough up in the form of pellets.

By carefully taking apart an owl pellet you can actually see what the owl has eaten. Sometimes you can find every bone from the animal the owl ate.

If you don't live near owls, ask at school or at a science center where you can buy an owl pellet.

WARNING MICROWAVE OWL PELLETS FOR MICROBIAL SAFETY! REMEMBER TO WASH YOUR HANDS WELL WHEN YOU'RE FINISHED AND BEFORE EATING!

For this experiment you'll also need some tweezers and newspapers.

1. Spread out some newspapers and get to work! Carefully use your tweezers to separate the fur and other materials from the bones. Set the bones aside.

2. Group the bones according to the drawings you see here. What bones did you find?

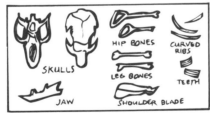

3. Which bones were easiest to identify? Were there any mysteries in what you found? Where might you get answers to your questions?

4. Observe the bones with your loupe and make a drawing of each one in your journal. How could you identify the animal your owl had eaten? This book may help you: *How Nature Works* by David Burnie (Pleasantville, NY: The Readers Digest Association, 1991).

5. Think about flight as a food-gathering strategy. What do owls eat? How can they successfully hunt those things they eat? What does flight enable them to do?

I'M FLYING!

How would you describe the concept of flying to someone from another planet? What words would you use? List these words and descriptions in your journal.

Have you ever had a dream about flying? Write and illustrate a poem about your own personal flying adventure.

FOR FURTHER EXPLORATION
Amazing Flying Machines by Robin Kerrod (New York: Knopf, 1992).
Kites on the Wind by Emery J. Kelly (Minneapolis, MN: Lerner, 1991).

SUPPORT NEEDED

Frameworks are important—whether it's a human skeleton, a bird's nest, or the outline for your next social studies report. A solid framework is strong, offers protection, and provides a place within which something can grow, whether it's a human being, baby birds, or your brilliant ideas!

Animal Clues

In designing building frameworks, we can take some lessons from the structure of animals and birds. Believe it or not, architects already have.

Compare, for example, the skeletal structure of a heavy animal like the elephant with that of an arched stone bridge. What similarities do you see? What other large animals have curved backs?

What about similarities in structure between birds and airplanes? skyscrapers and giraffes?

What other structural similarities between plants, animals, and architecture can you note in your journal?

Size Determines Shape

Size determines shape—in nature and in building structures. As the size increases, stronger materials must be used. The problem is, even the strongest material eventually will crumble under its own weight. What can be done? Think back to the previous chapters. What lessons might builders learn from

- the structure of birds' wings?
- the design and shape of birds' nests?
- the structure of pollen?
- the habits of crystals?

Write notes in your journal in the form of a memo of your recommendations.

Architects are challenged to produce structures that not only resist gravity, but which also can withstand

- all kinds of weather conditions;
- use by large numbers of people over many years; and
- wear and tear on the building materials over time.

CONCRETE ADVICE

The ancient Romans understood the idea of hollowed out construction. They placed hollow clay pots and pumice in the concrete when building the dome of the Pantheon.

Like birds' wings, building supports and beams are often hollowed out to reduce the overall weight. Even green peppers use this design principle. Cut one open and take a look! Look around. What other examples of hollowed out construction can you find?

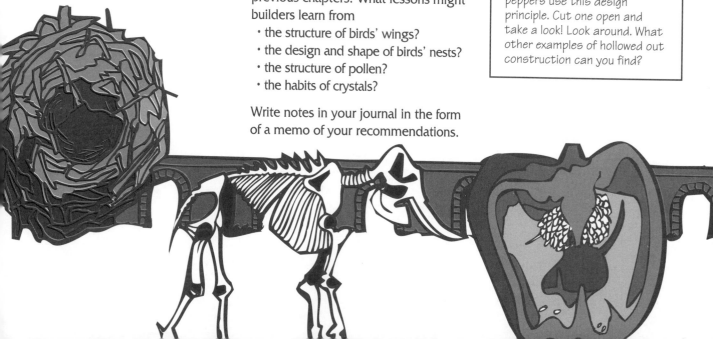

EXPERIMENT 1: IT'S A FRAME-UP!

SUPPLIES
2 boxes the same size (cereal boxes or macaroni and cheese)
2 lengths of string, each about 4-5 feet long
5 clip clothespins
a plywood board (about 12 inches by 24 inches)
2 screw-type cup hooks

Imagine being a bridge builder. You must build a structure that can withstand its own weight AND carry the weight of millions of vehicles and people over many years.

Suspension bridges are among the world's longest. They often span large bodies of water or cross deep canyons. Many are designed with two tall towers anchored in bedrock. See for yourself how these towers work.

1. Place the two boxes on their sides. Tie the string around each one so that they connect the two boxes.

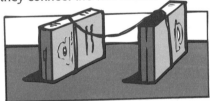

2. Carefully clip one clothespin at a time to the center of the string. What eventually happens to the boxes? Where is the weight focused? What would you have to do to improve the strength of your design?

Test this design improvement:

1. Screw the cup hooks into the board as shown. Tie one end of the string securely to one cup hook.

This time, simply drape the string over the books so it hangs down slightly in between them and tie the other end to the other hook.

2. Now clip a clothespin on the string where it hangs down between the books. What happens, and more important, why?

3. Look again at the drawing of the suspension bridge. What parts of the bridge do the books, hooks, and string in your model represent?

Triangles
Triangles are often used in bridge construction. Called **struts,** they provide lots of strength but less weight than solid construction. How many types of bridges use triangles for support?

What about vegetables and shells? Find a photo of the rain forest tree whose aboveground roots resemble struts. Examine the inside of a chicken leg bone. They also have little triangle "struts."

Since bridges can't "adapt" to changing conditions, designers often use mathematical models to test the strength and durability of their designs. They also build on the results of other successful and unsuccessful projects. If a bridge collapses, they can use that information in their future designs.

INVESTIGATE SOME MORE!

Have you heard the expression "strut your stuff"? Draw a picture of someone strutting, or better yet, demonstrate that kind of walk! How does strutting make you *feel*? Watch a friend strut. What impressions would you have of that person if you didn't know them? What feelings do you get from structures that have struts? Are there any similarities? What about differences?

EXPERIMENT 2: GOLDEN ARCHES

SUPPLIES
several encyclopedias (or other heavy books or square concrete blocks)
2 sheets of heavy construction paper
similar objects such as pennies

Curved arches have been popular for centuries. Look at some architecture books and notice the arches in historic cathedrals and bridges. Be on the lookout for some old and new arches in your own city (in addition to McDonald's, that is!).

Arches are decorative, but they are also strong. They're squeezed and pushed together by weight above and around them.

You can easily test the difference in strength between beam and arch construction.

Find a friend for this experiment. Each of you can build one bridge and compare.

1. Make two equal piles of books or blocks, each about 5" high. Leave about 8" in between the two piles.

2. Place one sheet of construction paper on top of the piles.

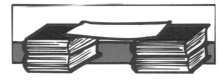

3. For the arched bridge, curve the second sheet of construction paper and place it in the opening as shown.

Where is the weight centered on each bridge? Which one do you think will hold the most weight? Why? Write your prediction in your journal.

4. Begin placing pennies in piles of five on each bridge at the same time. Did they both hold one pile? What about two? More? Which bridge do you think will last the longest? Why?

5. Which bridge collapsed first? Did the other bridge ever collapse? Record the results in your journal.

RAINBOW BRIDGE

Arches are not all made by people. Rainbow Bridge in Utah is a natural rock bridge that is 300 feet high at its center. How many grown-ups would need to stand on top of each other in order to reach the center of this bridge?

I DON'T KNOW ABOUT GROWN-UPS BUT ABOUT 1,800 BIG MACS COULD MAKE IT!

Arches are strong because they share the weight between supports, with the load-bearing part curving up in the middle for extra strength. It's the old elephant thing again.

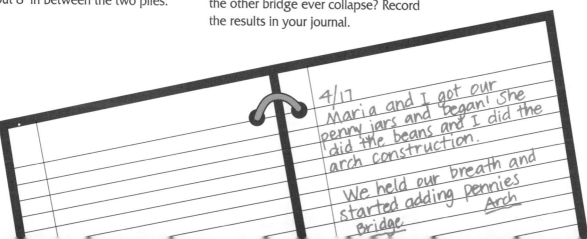

4/17
Maria and I got our penny jars and began! She did the beans and I did the arch construction.

We held our breath and started adding pennies. Arch Bridge

EXPLORE SOME MORE

TRIANGLE POWER

Try this simple experiment to test the strength of fan-folded paper.

1. Take two pieces of 8 1/2 x 11 construction paper. Fold one in approximately 9 fan folds as shown.

2. Place the folded paper lengthwise

so it spans two piles of books. Begin placing forks carefully on the paper in the space between the books. How many forks can you balance before the paper collapses?

3. Try the same thing with one piece of unfolded paper. How many forks does it take to collapse this "bridge"?

If you haven't already, take a look at the end of the fan-folded paper. What geometric shapes do you see? Now you see why corrugated paper is often a similar design. (**Hint:** What is corrugated paper used for?)

TOWERS OF POWER

Why are structures like the Great Pyramid, the Empire State Building, and the Eiffel Tower all skinnier at the top than at the bottom? Can you think of other famous or not-so-famous tall buildings that share this design?

Find ten of your dearest friends and build a similar structure with your bodies. How will you arrange yourselves? How many of you are at the bottom? How many are at the top? Who did you choose to be at the bottom and top? How did you decide? Who would definitely NOT be at the bottom? at the top? Why?

EXTRAORDINARY ANIMAL PLAY STRUCTURES

You have just won the coveted Kid's Favorite Architect award! No one is surprised. You managed to design an imaginative play structure that uses the structural elements of a specific animal or bird in its design. Kids everywhere love it. They're begging their parents to put one in their school playground, their neighborhood park, their backyard—their bedroom! How did you manage to come up with such an innovative design? Here's how.

1. First, choose your favorite animal, bird, fish, or reptile. Take your time in deciding, and even do a little research. When you know you have made the right choice, then design a fantastic play structure around one or more of those animals.

2. What unique parts of the animal will you incorporate into your structure? What materials will you use? What will kids particularly like?

3. Share your design. You can build a model, sketch it, or draw it on graph paper.

MY TOWN: A PHOTO ESSAY

Grab your camera and a role of black and white film. Make a list of interesting bridges, arches, and towers in your town. Take photos of them from different angles, at different times of the day, and in different kinds of weather conditions. Mount the best ones in a scrapbook alongside drawings of animals to show the similarities, or create a slide show of your work with text in the form of a poem to accompany the photos.

FOR FURTHER EXPLORATION
Bridges by Neil Ardley (Ada, OK: Garrett, 1990).
Bridges by Ken Robbins (New York: Dial, 1991).

GIVE ME SHELTER

Throughout history and the world, people have designed structures from available materials. They built houses to shelter them and protect them from the weather. Depending on where you live, the houses may be very different.

Here are some questions to start you thinking:

- Are there lots of wood frame houses where you live? Where in the world would you NOT want to use wood?

- Why do you think you find grass-roofed houses in many tropical climates?

- Why do people in the Arctic make houses from thick blocks of ice?

- Where is adobe used for building? What advantages does it have?

- Where in the world would you want a house on stilts, or a tepee or other structure that you could put up and take down easily?

One thing for certain. Wherever you live in the world, the houses you see are attempts to meet the needs of people. That is the essence of design.

In this chapter you will explore geodesic dome construction. You'll also have a chance to combine science and art as you design

- a fantasy house for an animal
- the perfect room for yourself or a friend
- a house or room for someone with a physical disability

DOGS KNOW BEST

Have you read about people who have survived in the wilderness in the winter by digging snow caves to keep themselves warm? Huskies know the same thing. These dogs dig caves in the snow the size of their bodies and curl up, using their body heat to warm the space.

EXPERIMENT 1: A DOME FOR A HOME

Geodesic domes, as you can see, take the idea of triangles to an extreme! Their whole construction, in fact, is based on them.

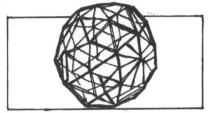

Think about what you discovered about strength in Chapter 9. How do geodesic domes rate in terms of strength and durability? Can you think of any disadvantages?

You can experiment with geodesic dome structures very easily. . . and deliciously! This is a fun activity for a birthday party, sleepover, or camping trip.

There is one big problem. What will you do with your structure when you're all done? I'm sure you'll think of something. (**Hint:** Don't forget the graham crackers and chocolate bars.)

Geodesic domes come in many different sizes and shapes. Use this model to get you started.

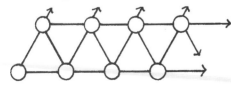

1. Enlarge your template onto a piece of 8 1/2 x 13 paper. The circles are marshmallows; the lines are toothpicks. To begin, you might want to place your marshmallows (or gumdrops) and toothpicks directly on the template.

2. Here are some important questions to consider as you build your dome:

• How will you make your dome curve?

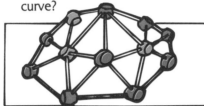

• How does your structure feel in your hands as you go along? What happens to its strength each time you connect more triangles?

Be warned! You may be inspired to design a very unique geodesic structure. If so, great! With lots of structures together, you and your friends can create a whole community.

Throughout the process, keep notes about your questions, hunches, and discoveries in your journal, just as a scientist would. Add further notes and sketches as you go along.

I WONDER. . .
What would it take to make a life-size dome playhouse? What materials would you use?

I COULD START WITH MARSHMALLOWS BUT I DON'T THINK THEY COME THAT LARGE!

FUTURE SITE OF MY DOME PLAYHOUSE

DID YOU KNOW?
The overall structure of a dome is similar to certain microscopic viruses.

THE FATHER OF DOMES
Read about Buckminster Fuller, the father of geodesic domes, in the library or an online encyclopedia. He believed that triangles were stronger than cube-shaped buildings. In domes the weight is squeezed and pushed in all directions.

EXPERIMENT 2: A TWO-PART DESIGN PROJECT

Throughout this book, you've looked at structures of different kinds. You have seen how the use, or function, of a structure often influences its form.

If you can, find a copy of the book, *Need a House? Call Ms. Mouse!* by George Mendoza (New York: Grosset & Dunlap, 1981).

In this book, architect Henrietta Mouse designs the perfect house for 14 of her friends, who include a cat, fish, squirrel, frog, pig, and otter. To do this, Henrietta has to understand the basic needs of her clients, what they enjoy, and what they require in their ideal living space.

Take what you've learned about structure and function and put it to work as Henrietta's trusted partner!

Part 1: Animal House

Design the perfect model house for the animal of your choice. To do this you will need to answer some questions:

HELLO... MS. MOUSE? I NEED HELP WITH A HOUSE!

- Where does this animal live?
- What does it need to survive?
- What would it like included in its ideal living space?
- What materials will you use?

What else might you want to know?

Look around for materials you can use to construct your model house. As the architect, when it's finished, write a short description telling why you made the design decisions you did.

Part 2: Home Sweet Home

Now it's time to design the ultimate room for yourself or a friend! Use the same process above. If you and a friend work together, interview each other and then design the perfect room based on the information you've collected. Here are some ideas to guide your interview:

DIRTY CLOTHES

- Size issues (Are you tired of some things being too high/too low for you? How can you allow for growth? Are there any other physical considerations you want to keep in mind?)

- Your basic needs (What basic needs do you have? Which of these needs should your room meet?)

- Your interests (How will your interests—in art, science, music, animals, sports, for example—influence the design of your room?)

10/1
INTERVIEW WITH ANDY
Size:
Andy needs a longer bed and a desk he can fit his legs underneath! - Room to practice his drums.
Interests:
Good lighting, built-in sound proofing.

THREE LITTLE PIGS REVISITED

Maybe that pig wasn't so foolish after all. Today, there is renewed excitement over straw bale construction for houses and barns. Straw bale construction saves energy and trees, provides good insulation, and is low in cost. Surprisingly, it's also resistant to fire and earthquakes.

In this building method, large bales of straw are reinforced with steel rods that anchor it to the foundation. The bales are laid like bricks in an interlocking pattern, finished with stucco on the outside, and plaster and paint on the inside.

Some people wonder how straw bale buildings would hold up in a climate where there is a lot of rain. What do you think? What other questions do you have about straw bale construction? How could you design an experiment to test one of your questions?

DESIGNING WITH PEOPLE IN MIND

Do you have a physical disability, or do you know someone who does? For people with disabilities, narrow hallways, high counters, stairs, drinking fountains, and many bathrooms can be serious barriers.

To raise your awareness of this issue, here are some things you can do:

1. Take a notebook and walk around your house, school, and neighborhood. What places would not be accessible in a wheelchair?

2. Interview someone in your school or community who is in a wheelchair. What are the biggest problems in their environment? What suggestions do they have for builders and designers?

3. Armed with your increased awareness, choose one room in your house or school, and redesign it with wheelchair access in mind. What would it take to make your house or school more accessible to people with physical disabilities? Make a list of specific recommendations and include some sketches if necessary.

DESIGNER AWARD

You have been given the job of handing out the top Design Award of the century. There are two candidates: Mother Nature and Humankind. Who will get the award for the best designer? Think back on what you've examined in this book.

Use your journal to collect your thoughts on the arguments you will use to support your opinion. Find a friend who has the opposite viewpoint and listen carefully to each other's views. What are the best arguments for each choice?

VOLUNTEER IN YOUR COMMUNITY

It wouldn't be right to end this book without remembering that there are many children and adults who do not have a home. Maybe you and your friends can take your scientific spirit out into the community. Volunteer to find out more about homelessness in your town, what's being done about the problem, and what you can do to help.

Sometimes science is active, roll-up-your-sleeves kind of work. You don't have to be grown up to make a difference in the world.

FOR FURTHER EXPLORATION

Round Buildings, Square Buildings, & Buildings That Wiggle Like a Fish by Philip M. Isaacson (New York: Knopf, 1990).

What It Feels Like to Be a Building by Forrest Wilson (Washington, DC: The Preservation Press, 1988).

Kids Explore the Gifts of Children with Special Needs by the Westridge Young Writers Workshop (Santa Fe, NM: John Muir Publications, 1994).

GLOSSARY

Bernoulli's principle a theory that says the faster a liquid or gas moves, the less pressure it has

capillary action the pulling or pushing forces of a liquid up or down a tube due to cohesion, adhesion, and surface tension

cartilage an elastic connective tissue that lines joints and cushions bones to reduce friction

chromatography the process used to separate different substances in a mixture

cohesion the force of attraction between two particles which holds a substance together

crystallography the scientific study of the form, structure, and physical and chemical properties of crystals

dispersal to send and scatter in different directions

endoskeleton the internal skeleton or framework of a creature

exoskeleton the external skeleton or shell of a creature

invertebrates creatures that have no backbones

leaf skeleton the framework of a leaf whose green tissue is removed

lift the upward force that keeps airplanes and birds in the air

mollusks the largest group of invertebrates that live in the sea, in fresh water, and on land

penicillium a group of fungi usually found as a blue-green mold on bread, cheese, and other nonliving organic matter

photosynthesis the method that plants use to make food from water and carbon dioxide, using the sun's energy

samaras dry fruit whose winglike seed structures help their dispersal by the wind

skeleton the network of bones and cartilage in vertebrates that support the body; the framework of a building

stalactites calcite deposits that hang down from the ceilings and walls of caves

stalagmites calcite deposits that grow upward from the floors of caves

struts support pieces used to resist pressure or thrust in architectural structure

surface tension the force of liquid molecules that cling together to form an elastic skinlike film across the surface of a liquid

transpiration a plant's loss of water through evaporation

vertebrates creatures that have backbones